LIGHTBRINGERS and LAMPLIGHTERS

A young man's journey of learning

DOC LIST

2018

AnotherThought Inc.

COPYRIGHT

DEDICATION

I have been the beneficiary of many valuable influences in my life. While I could readily dedicate this to my father, Murray List, or my darling wife, Debbie List, I've decided that the most significant influence in my life, in the context of this book, is my mother, Diana Roberta Gellman List Cullen.

My mother demonstrated a lifelong fascination with learning new ideas and ways of doing and being. She was endlessly curious, and shared her fascination and her curiosity with me. We were able to have long, open, interesting conversations, which was a blessing.

I miss her, remember her clearly and joyfully, and remain influenced by her every day of my life.

CONTENTS

FOREWORD

The purpose of a foreword, as I understand it, is to help the reader decide whether or not to read the book. Since no author would include a foreword that advised against reading the book, it's fair to admit right here that I like this book and think you should read it. But there were issues, at least for me. Here's the story:

Despite my fearsome good looks and curmudgeonly demeanor, I am actually pretty friendly when approached, rarely biting and only occasionally even scratching or snarling. I try to emulate my cat in that. And, as with my cat, there aren't all that many people whom I actually want to know better: I'm open to it but don't seek it.

Doc List is someone you'd like to know better. When you meet him in person, you like him because he's interesting and he's interested in you. You start feeling good about yourself for some reason. Maybe this should be a bit scary, but somehow it isn't.

Even though every time I'd encountered him, he had a camera in his hands and was taking pictures, I was still surprised to find that his Twitter feed is almost entirely made up of photos, beautiful photos, often with just a few words that take you right into the picture. Words that make you think. I like the pictures, and the little thoughts they bring.

When you like a person's work, you start to like them more and want to know them better. So when Doc asked me to write a foreword for this book, I was favorably inclined and dug right in reading it. The good news is that it's an easy read.

The bad news, and he tells you this right up front, is that it's an allegory.

An allegory. You know, one of those stories with a not particularly hidden meaning, that they made you read in school and then write a few paragraphs showing that you got the meaning and were enlightened. Allegories are often uplifting. They usually involve some naive character starting out in a bad place, traveling around, stumbling, getting in trouble, until at the end, discovery, learning, insight. Naive character gains insight, so does reader, write paragraphs, collect grade.

If I'm not reading something technical, I'm reading fiction. I like fiction about competent people, space men and women, detectives, adventurers. People I could want to be. Competent people, sure, going through something tough, coming out on top. I was always a nebbishy dweeb in real life, and I never liked reading about them. Allegories are always about some nebbishy dweeb, so they don't get a very large shelf in my library.

Well, this one goes on my small allegory shelf. Having said I'd consider writing a foreword, I dove in to read it. I read it right through. It's an easy read, a nice little story, and it went along more or less as I expected. There are some clear signals that it's an allegory ... and there are odd bits that make you wonder. I honestly found the book rather engaging, certainly interesting enough to keep on reading.

Then I got to the end. The book ends in a perfectly reasonable way, with a perfectly reasonable happy ending. I like books with good conclusions and happy endings. It all went more or less as you'd expect. Except for this:

This little book actually made me think. Not the doing your homework, write your three paragraphs kind of think. Somehow, the book really applied to me. It asked me questions about myself, and told me things about myself. It made me think, and gave me valuable positive insight into myself.

You'd like Doc List because he is interesting and interested in you.

I think you'll like this book because, like Doc, it's interested in you. I don't even know how it's possible for a book to be interested in you. This one is.

Give it a chance to know you.

...Ron Jeffries

...ronjeffries.com

PREFACE

The inspiration for this book came to me in a flash while watching the movie "The Lion, the Witch, and the Wardrobe" from the book of the same name by C. S. Lewis. The story is about four children who all ultimately step through the wardrobe into a fantastic world, in which they have adventures.

There's a scene early in the movie in which Lucy - the youngest - is exploring an area covered in snow. Lucy comes upon a small snow-covered clearing in the middle of which is a lamppost topped by a gas lamp. At that moment, while watching the movie, the idea for this book came to me almost full-blown.

I can't explain it. I don't want to or need to. The next day I began writing. I was unusually disciplined throughout the writing of this book, setting aside a specific time each day to write. It was a marvelous experience. The book just seemed to write itself through my brain and hands.

I have re-read this book many times. I have edited it, put it aside, and re-edited it. I have gone for long periods without touching it and then re-reading it again.

Recently I showed the latest version to my friend Sweet Van Loan. After reading it she said: "I love it! This was (truly) wonderful to read!

I really couldn't put it down after Chapter 13! I love the humor and the Quest. YOU NEED TO WRITE MORE BOOKS!

"And this FOR SURE needs to be a physical book and maybe an eBook, too?"

That was the trigger for the action.

I hope you enjoy this book. I hope you enjoy it as much as Sweet did. I enjoy it every time I read it, and frequently find myself thinking "I wrote this?"

INTRODUCTION

This is an allegory. It's the story of Ham the Huddler, and what happens to him and his journey of discovery. It's about ideas and limitations and self-imposed restrictions.

At least, I think that's what it's about.

At least one of my friends in the agile software development community told me that it was about agile. Or something like that.

From where I sit, it's about whatever you think it's about.

Now, on to Lightbringers and Lamplighters.

PROLOGUE

"It is time," said the first voice.

.."Do you really think so?" asked a second voice.

…."Indeed, it is time," said a third.

.."And how shall we proceed?" asked the second voice.

"A child has been born," said the first voice, "and chosen. He will
serve our purposes quite nicely."

…."He will know the purpose, and recognize the time, even if he
does not know the why of it," said the third voice.

.."So be it," said the second voice.

And there was silence and agreement and it was begun.

CHAPTER 01

H am felt the sweat dripping down his back as he swung the axe overhead. In his mind's eye, he could see the sweat clearing a path through the dirt and dust that settled on his back as he worked. He took some pride in the smooth play of the muscles in his shoulders, chest, and back as he continued to split logs for firewood for the village. Each time was the same – place the log end up on the splitting trunk, take the axe firmly – first with his left hand, then with his right – swing the axe around his right side and overhead, and then the solid, smooth swing downward ending in the satisfying *ka-thunk* as the log split in two.

Ham had been splitting firewood since he was old enough to swing his first, smaller axe, and it had always given him a quiet sense of satisfaction. His father had taught him the right way to grip the axe, the right way to swing it up and then down, the right way to place the log, and the rhythm that made it all move so smoothly.

On this day, as on most other days, his father – Horace – worked at his own splitting trunk not far away. Their rhythms worked in counterpoint to make a calming rhythm. Ka-thunk, ka-thunk, sometimes together, sometimes apart.

The work took no thought, so Ham used the time when his body worked so smoothly to think. This was one of the things that set Ham apart from the other Huddlers of the village of Dusk. In fact, Ham had always felt somewhat apart from the other Huddlers of Dusk.

To begin with, Ham had always been a bit taller than most Huddlers. Not head-and-shoulders taller, but just enough that he was always looking down on the other Huddlers. Because of the physical nature of his work, Ham's shoulders began broadening early, and his back was strong and straight. All of this made him seem just a bit taller than he already was.

Ham's hair was different, too. Huddlers, as a people, had lifeless muddy brown hair that always seemed to just lay there. Whether the day was calm or windy, Huddler hair found its place and gloomily stayed there. By contrast, Ham's hair had a sheen – a slight golden tinge to it that seemed to catch every errant sunbeam or moonglow. So much so, that the other Huddlers in Dusk could see him coming from a distance. Not content to stay put, Ham's hair moved with the breeze and flowed in the light.

And then, there were Ham's eyes. Possessed of a warm radiance, they were like the eyes of the other Huddlers, only in that they were brown. But while the other Huddlers' eyes were a muddy brown just like their muddy brown hair, Ham's eyes were brighter. Sometimes, in the right light, small, floating golden flecks appeared.

Unfortunately for Ham, different was bad in Dusk. The folk of Dusk mistrusted different, as did most of the folk in the land of Dank.

The other children of Dusk avoided Ham in small and large ways. Sometimes, when he would walk by, they would just turn away, ever so slightly. At playtime, they would often deliberately exclude him.

Ham was never bitter or angry, but these slights did not go unnoticed and there had always been a small sadness in him.

As Ham chopped wood, this sadness would sometimes sing a soft song to him. As Ham smelled the rich scent of the wood, feeling the smooth play of his muscles and the sweat dripping down his back to plop in the dirt at his feet, he would listen and wonder why he was different.

CHAPTER 02

Ham's village of Dusk was a part of the land of Dank. In Dank, it was always dim and dreary. The sun, when it managed to peek through the ever-present overcast, was weak, wan and woeful. The inhabitants of Dank – the Huddlers – went through their days with their heads down, their shoulders hunched, and with a look of fear and anxiety shrouding their faces from waking to sleeping. Whenever possible – when they weren't working, schooling, or doing chores – they would spend their time together, huddled against the darkness. And their dreams were, as you might imagine, dark, dim and dreary.

For the most part, Huddlers spent their time on the necessities of life: growing and gathering food, patching together clothing, fixing leaks in the roofs of their homes. As much as possible, they did their chores together, huddled, feeling hopeless.

Nothing ever changed in the land of Dank. The Huddlers lived in the homes that their parents and grandparents and great-grandparents had lived in. They grew and gathered their food from the same fields and trees and in the same way as the generations before them. When one of their homes was damaged, they used the same tools, in the same way, to make repairs. No one had had a new idea, or come up with a new way of doing things, in living memory. And the Huddlers had very good memories. Of course, they didn't have a lot to remember, since things just didn't change.

CHAPTER 03

H yram was Mayor of Dusk. Hyram was Mayor because his father had been Mayor, and his father's father had been Mayor, and so on.

Hyram was an average looking Huddler: average height, mousy brown hair that lay where it fell and stayed there, brown watery eyes that mostly looked down, and a bit of a pot-belly – the kind that looked like he'd swallowed a medium-sized melon and it got stuck.

Hyram was responsible for enforcing the laws of Dusk, providing wise counsel to the Huddlers of Dusk, and overseeing the well-being of the community of Dusk. There weren't many laws, of course, since things hadn't changed much. Hyram's wise counsel wasn't in great demand, since the denizens of Dusk knew pretty much everything there was to know about life in their village.

Most of the time, Hyram huddled with his fellow denizens of Dusk, looking fearfully at the surrounding dim, dark dreariness. Once in a while, he had to resolve a petty dispute. At those times, Hyram relied on the knowledge that had come down to him from generations of Dusk Huddlers. Actually, the Huddlers of Dusk knew what Hyram knew, but they liked to make Hyram feel good about himself now and then.

On those rare occasions when Hyram was called upon to decide an issue, he would always take a deep breath, draw back his shoulders, and begin with "Hrmmmmmm…" His eyes would bulge a bit, as though the pressure building up in his head was about to push out through his eyes.

This didn't happen often.

CHAPTER 04

Life was dull in Dusk. Entertainment was rare, and usually took the form of singing the Birthday Dirge. Everyone knows the Birthday Dirge. It goes like this...

"Hap... py birth... day... to... youuuuuuuuu...

Hap... py birth... day... to... youuuuuuuu..."

And so on. Slow, mournful, as though each reminder of another year passed is just another year of collecting dust, approaching death, and dragging dreariness. And that's the best that the Huddlers of Dusk could manage for entertainment.

Work was just work for the Huddlers. Repetitive. The Huddlers of Dusk did what they needed to do to feed and clothe themselves and keep their homes from leaking or falling down. They didn't sing or whistle while they worked, because they didn't find any real joy in what they were doing. In fact, it's not at all clear that anyone in Dusk knew how to whistle.

Huddlers learned what to do from their parents, who had learned from their parents, who had learned from... And they did it the same way, day after day, week after week, month after month, year after year.

There was no innovation in Dusk.

CHAPTER 05

Ham lived with his mother, Hannah, and his father, Horace. Their home was a typical Huddler home, with packed dirt floors, cast iron sinks, off-white walls, thatched roof, and an oh-my-goodness-that's-chilly toilet. Along with Hannah, Horace, and Ham, there was Ham's sister Helen and their dog – a mutt of unknown origin – Hank.

Ham's family was like most of the other Huddler families in Dusk. When not splitting wood, Horace gathered food, did repairs and maintenance around their small home, and occasionally shared his woes with some of the other husbands and fathers in the village. Hannah washed their clothes (although they were so overall drab and dingy that you might never know), cooked their meals (which all seemed to look and taste very much alike), and cared for their occasional ills.

Helen, a youngster of 15, went to the one-room schoolhouse with the other children of Dusk, dragging her feet and her books all the way there and back. There wasn't a lot to learn, but they all went to school because... well, because. She never could figure it out.

Ham was different. No one could account for it, since there hadn't been anyone or anything different in Dusk in the long memories of the denizens of Dusk. And yet, at 21, Ham was different.

Ham was one of the few imaginative Huddlers, occasionally having a vision of something more. When the sun made one of its rare appearances, Ham would tell his friends and neighbors the tale of his vision.

CHAPTER 06

As far back as he could remember Ham had had the same dream. While this was just one more thing that set him apart, he nonetheless would share the dream with other Huddlers from time to time.

"One day, a man comes to Dusk. Since no one ever comes to Dusk, everyone comes out into the center of the village to see. This man strides into Dusk. Since we all kind of shuffle along from thing to thing, striding causes a stir, and everyone starts to whisper and mumble.

"And then we notice that this man is tall. Not just a little bit taller, not just enough so that your eyes are looking at his nose, but tall. His chin is just about at the spot between my eyes, and since I'm just a bit taller than everyone else, that makes him tall.

"As he stands there and we're all staring at him, the sun blasts through the clouds, so bright we can almost hear it. As if this wasn't enough to make everyone stand still and silent, the light slaps the man on the head and we see red. Not brown – not mousy brown or dirt brown or tree-bark-brown or muddy brown – but red. Shocking red, shouting red, stunning red.

"And then the man smiles. Oh, how white his teeth are. How wide his smile. How joyful and bright and uplifting that smile is. As I look at him, I know that he is here to bring us something new, something that will change our lives in ways we can't even imagine.

"The man looks at each of us. I mean he really looks at each of us, one by one. As he looks, we each see that his eyes are golden, shining, and it feels as if there's a private connection from his eyes to each of ours. I watch as he looks around at the Huddlers of Dusk, one by one, and I see each of you start to smile. Each of you stands up just a little taller and your hair seems to glow just a little bit, and your shoulders go back just a little bit.

"He opens his mouth to speak, and we all hold our breath and lean forward just a bit and…"

This is the point where Ham's dream ends. He's had the dream more than once, and each time, it ends at this point.

Ham is both frustrated and excited. He knows that there's something important in this dream. He knows that if he can just hear what the man is going to say that the lives of all the Huddlers in Dusk will be changed forever.

Sometimes, when Ham thinks of the dream, he cries in frustration.

The other Huddlers of Dusk, each time they hear Ham tell of his dream, shake their heads, mumble into their hands, and shuffle away.

CHAPTER 07

Strangely, Ham's dream seemed to give him some joy. It's not strange that the dream would give him joy except that joy was so rare in Dusk. As we know, the Huddlers didn't celebrate much and didn't get excited about much and pretty much every day was like every other day so what was there to get joyful about?

And yet, Ham had these moments of joy. You could always tell with Ham, because his frown disappeared and the gold sparkles in his eyes seemed more noticeable and his hair seemed to have just a slight extra ripple at those times.

If Ham was walking somewhere, when he was thinking about his dream, he would look straight ahead or even up instead of down at the ground, as most of the Huddlers did, and as Ham did most of the time. If you listened closely, you might hear a strange sound coming from Ham – something like humming, although no one quite knew what the sound was since they had never heard it before.

One day, the strangest thing happened. Ham was walking through the center of Dusk, as were a number of the other Huddlers of Dusk. As usual, Ham and the others were shuffling along, heads down, not talking or coughing or laughing. As usual, the day was somewhat overcast, the weather wasn't really warm or cold or wet or dry, just drab. As usual, no one really looked at anyone else or talked to anyone else.

And then it happened... the sun peeked through the overcast, and seemed to throw a beam of light straight at Ham. As it reached toward him, it seemed that the golden highlights in his hair reached out and gathered the paltry bit of light to themselves and gleamed. Ham found himself standing in a spot that was just slightly lighter, just slightly warmer, just slightly gentler than his surroundings, and he stopped stock still. He looked up, and for the first time that anyone could remember, his eyes sparkled, and the golden flecks seemed to move a bit.

And Ham spoke! No one ever spoke while walking through the village. What was there to speak about? Life was the same, day after day, drab, dreary, dingy, dull. Not today – Ham spoke!

"I get it!"

That's all he said. The other Huddlers of Dusk stopped momentarily, looked up, looked at each other, and then – as one – they shrugged and went back to shuffling along, eyes down, silently.

CHAPTER 08

Not even Ham knew for certain what it was that he "got". As he'd been standing in that lost ray of gentle sunlight, Ham had connected his dream to his circumstances. He found himsel believing in something new, for a Huddler. That new thing was the word "Lightbringer."

As Ham drank in that small draught of sunlight, that word had sprung to mind and Ham believed that he knew – to a certainty – what his dream meant. He couldn't quite put it into words, but he knew – as he knew his name and he knew he lived in Dank and he knew his father's name was Horace and his mother's name was Hannah – he knew that the man in his vision was real, and that he had to find him to learn what it all meant.

In that moment, Ham began planning for a journey to find the man in his vision.

This is such an exceptional thing, that it bears pondering and patting and playing with. No one in Dusk, no one in the entire land of Dank, as far as Ham knew, had ever gone on a quest. No one had ever talked about having a vision, in fact, much less going on a quest because of a vision. And there was Ham, mentally preparing to go on a quest to seek a man who might or might not exist.

Having no one to whom he could turn for help or guidance, Ham began to do something that had never before been done.

First, Ham had to think about what it meant to go on a quest. Since he didn't own a horse (not many folks in Dank did), Ham pictured himself walking. Since no one he knew had ever walked out of Dusk, the image in his head got very hazy after leaving the immediate surroundings of the village. Mostly, he just saw himself, as though looking down from above, trudging along a narrow strip of dirty, dusty ground.

Ham continued on his way that day. As he went from place to place, he thought more about his journey.

"I'll need water," he thought. "How will I carry water with me?" He looked around the village of Dank, with the idea of carrying water in his head. Each container, sack, cup, or bottle he saw he considered as a vessel for carrying water. The day after that errant ray of light changed his life forever, Ham found what he needed in his own home. For all of his life his family had kept their supply of water for drinking and cooking in a tube-shaped bag with a large opening at one end where they could pour in water from a bucket at the well, and a stoppered opening at the other end where they could let water out when they needed it. He saw, by looking carefully at that tube-shaped bag, that he could attach a piece of rope and sling the bag over his shoulder and carry it with him. Of course, if he did that, his family would no longer have a way to keep their water in their home.

And at that moment, Ham stepped from thinking the unthought to doing the undone. He set out to make another water bag just like the one in his home. He found the materials, sought out the water bag maker, learned out how to put the materials together, and made his own water bag for traveling.

As he went through this process, the other Huddlers of Dusk began to take notice. After all, Ham was not a water bag maker. Chicken pluckers plucked chickens, well diggers dug wells, farmers farmed, and water bag makers made water bags. Ham was not a water bag maker, and yet he was making a water bag!

Even the dull and discouraged Huddlers of Dusk were stirred by this change, even so small a change. One – Hyram, the Mayor of Dusk, as it happens – went so far as to have a conversation with Ham about it.

"What are you doing, Ham?"

"Hullo, Hyram. I'm making a water bag."

"But you're not a water bag maker, Ham."

"Hmm – yes, you're right, Hyram. But I needed a water bag, and we don't have any extras in Dank, and Herman the water bag maker only makes new ones when one wears out."

This was a long soliloquy for a Huddler!

Hyram thought about this for a while. It was like a bit of gristle that – no matter how long and hard he chewed – just wouldn't get soft enough or small enough to swallow. So Hyram just spit out the whole idea, and went back to life as usual.

Almost.

Because somewhere in Hyram's Huddler head, the idea of making and learning something new had settled like dandelion fluff and was there for the long haul.

CHAPTER 09

Each day found Ham either making something for his journey, or thinking of what he needed.

Consider… the Huddlers of Dusk did the same things, day after day. They lived the same way as their parents and grandparents and great-grandparents. The chicken plucker came from a long line of chicken pluckers. The farmers came from long lines of farmers. And the water bag maker came from a long line of water bag makers.

Ham's long line was starting to look like a drunken snake wandering along a bumpy path, going this way and that, looping about and finding its way without any seeming purpose. But the purpose was there. Ham was on a journey from here to somewhere.

Each twist and loop and bump in Ham's path resulted in something he needed for his journey…

A pack for his food.

Something to sleep in.

Something to keep the rain off.

Extra clothes.

A pack to carry it all in.

After a few weeks of preparation, Ham realized that the picture in his head had changed. No longer did he see himself in just the clothes on his back trudging along a dusty dirt track into the hazy unknown. Now he saw himself walking erect, with his head up, his pack on his back, his water bag slung over his shoulder, and his eyes pointed straight ahead.

In just those few weeks, Ham had found something new within himself. He knew that it came from his vision and the gift of that stray and unexpected bump of sunlight, and he knew that it was all about his determination to find the man in his vision.

During those weeks, Ham had learned the skills and knowledge of others. This was not bad – there were no rules against learning the skills and knowledge of others. It was just different. It just wasn' done in the village of Dusk in the land of Dank.

The other Huddlers of Dusk had become uncomfortable. They began to mumble and grumble to each other a bit more each day.

"Ham did what?"

"…see what Ham made?"

"Ham said what?"

Through this time, Ham found that he had one absolute gift – certainty.

Certainty is a remarkable thing, especially when based on belief The object of that belief doesn't matter, so much as the fact of tha belief. And Ham had it.

CHAPTER 10

On a typical Dank morning, when the sky was overcast and the weather was dreary, Ham was ready.

He had extra clothes.

He had his water bag, and it was filled with water.

He had his food pack, and it was packed with food.

He had his sleeping roll and his weather shield and his pack in which to carry it all.

He was ready.

Ham put his food pack and his extra clothes and his sleeping roll and his weather shield in his pack, slung his pack and his water bag over his shoulder and looked around the family home he had known all of his life.

He looked at Horace, his father, and said "It's time for me to go." They embraced briefly.

He walked to Hannah, his mother, and putting his arms around her said "I will find him, and then I will know." Hannah looked in his face, stroked his hair, and nodded.

He hugged Helen, his sister, and whispered "The Lightbringer." She looked at him with a combination of fear and awe, wrapped him tightly in her arms, and then let him go.

He patted Hank, their dog, and savored a last lick and lap.

Ham walked through the center of Dusk, as he had in the picture in his head. As he walked through the village, the Huddlers of Dusk huddled together. In some strange way, they seemed frightened.

Ham had learned the skills of others. He had thought the unthought and done the undone. And now he was doing something more that was never thought of or done until that day – he was leaving Dusk.

None of the Huddlers of Dusk had ever left. They grew up, married the Huddler that was chosen for them to marry, had baby Huddlers, and lived the lives and did the work that their parents and grandparents and great-grandparents had done before them.

None of them ever left until today, that is. Ham left.

Ham walked to the edge of the village of Dusk, a little more erect and confident than he felt. This was as far as he'd ever come in his life. Everything that was a part of his life was within the boundaries of the village. Farms and workshops and homes and animals and tools and all the people of Dusk were inside those boundaries.

Ham stood at the edge. At that moment, his confidence and certainty were tested. He took a moment to question his belief.

"Is there a man, a Lightbringer, out there somewhere? No one in Dusk has ever stepped past the village borders, and here I stand about to step off. Is it worth it? Can I handle it?"

Ham stood while the sun stepped slowly, inch by inch, up the sky, banging and bumping at the clouds covering Dusk and the land of Dank. Ham looked at the ground, as any good Huddler would.

Then Ham lifted his eyes and looked straight ahead, into the world beyond Dusk. He saw nothing frightening. He felt unease, but no fear. Finally Ham tipped his neck and head back and looked up at the overcast drear of the sky, and saw the slightest hint of the sun and he knew, once again.

Ham took his first step out of Dusk, and began his journey.

CHAPTER 11

Nothing happened except a small puff of dust as Ham's foot planted itself in the soil. There were no cheers or applause, nor boos or catcalls. There was just the slightest mumble behind him.

Ham turned and looked over his shoulder back into the village of Dusk, and he saw figures huddled at the corners of the buildings. They just looked, and a few mumbled to others.

"Outside?"

"Leaving Dusk?"

"Where…?"

With his second step Ham was outside of Dusk. For the first time in his memory, and in fact in the memory of the oldest Huddler elders, someone was outside of Dusk. Ham had just a hint, at that moment, of the importance of this occasion. Do not forget that Ham was a Huddler, a people who are not renowned for their deep thought, terrific insight, or emotional range. So while Ham did have the slightest sense of something important, mostly he just started walking.

He wondered, as he left Dusk, why there seemed to be a road leaving Dusk if no one ever left Dusk. It was clear to Ham that this was not an entirely natural cleared space that led off in front of him.

The road led east. The hint of sun was in front of and above Ham as he walked. As he walked, he rolled the word "Lightbringer" around in his mind.

He knew that he hadn't made up that word. It was as if it had just appeared in his mind on the day that the sun stroked him for just that wonderful moment. He just wasn't sure quite what it meant, or why it was so significant.

Looking around just a bit as he walked – being a Huddler, even an unusual one, his curiosity wasn't great – Ham saw that he was walking on a bare stripe running between forests and fields. The trees in the forests were somewhat droopy and drab. The fields were dirty and dusty, with just the barest bit of dull grass struggling to make a good showing.

"Why is it all the same? And why so drear and drab and dull?"

And so it went, through the morning. Ham walked, looking and thinking as he went. Occasionally a plain brown bird would flap by, or a discouraged deer would thump across his path. Generally, it was pretty unremarkable.

Around noon, when the hint of a glow of the sun was pretty much over his head, Ham came to a large rock by the side of the road. The rock was a bit wider across than Ham was tall, and about the height of his knees. This was the perfect place to stop, sit, eat, and maybe take a short rest.

Ham sat and had his lunch of brown bread and bean paste, a bruised apple, and a sip of water from his water bag. Finishing his lunch, Ham lay down on the rock, which was warmer than the air, and quickly fell asleep.

Ham dreamt. In his dream, he was walking down the road toward the east. He came to a village, and he asked the people "Have you seen the Lightbringer?" The answer was always the same: "What is a Lightbringer?" He left and continued on to one village after another, always asking "Have you seen the Lightbringer?" and always getting the same answer.

Ham awoke. He had expected to see the Lightbringer in his dream, not to dream of the futility of his search. But Ham still had that one sure gift, the gift of certainty founded on belief. So he put on his backpack, slung his water bag over his shoulder, stood up, and continued his journey east.

CHAPTER 12

Ham's journey, on that first day, was mostly uneventful. He saw more drab trees and dusty fields. There were rock-colored rocks and dun-colored birds and dusty and discouraged dee and that was about it.

Ham walked mostly with his head down, watching as the dust rose with each step. By mid-afternoon, his shoes and his stockings and his pants were well dusted with the history of his journey thus far. Of course, since his clothes were pretty much a dirt-brown color, you couldn't tell unless you looked closely.

There was grit everywhere. It was between his teeth, grinding as he walked, and in his eyes, scritching behind his eyelids as he blinked. There was dust and dirt in his hair, in the seams of his pockets, and under his fingernails.

Toward the end of the afternoon, Ham heard the gentlest burbling mumbling sound. He lifted his head and his eyes, and for the first time since his nap on the stone at noon, he looked around with some interest. At first, he saw only more drab trees and dusty fields. And yet there was that tickling, taunting hint of a burble, and Ham knew there must be a stream somewhere nearby.

While he looked and listened, Ham thought about his life in Dusk. At the moment, his thoughts turned to the question of bathing, as the dust and grit worked its way into every seam of his clothes and every aperture of his body. In Dusk, the youngest member of the family would go to the well at the center of the village every morning. That person, be it child or adult, would fetch back two buckets of water for drinking and cooking, plus one additional bucket of water for each person in the home to use for bathing and washing. In the morning, each person in the home would splash some chilly water over face and hands and rinse out his or her mouth. At noon, each person having worked through the morning, they would repeat this ritual before eating.

In the evening, though, was the best time in the drab life of Dusk. At sunset, the remaining washing water would be warmed in a large pot over the fire. The pot would be left over the fire while each member of the household had some private time to bathe with their share of the heated water. No one ever took more than their share of time or water – it just wasn't done, and no one in Dusk (or, probably, in the entire land of Dank) ever considered taking more than their share.

Ham reflected on the small pleasure of bathing in warm water each evening as he walked and listened for the burblemumble of the stream. With his head lifted, his eyes roaming around, and his nose sniffing, Ham came around a curve in the path and found himself looking straight at a stream cutting across his path.

Ham had never seen a stream before. Well, at least not one large enough to cut across a path. In Dusk there was a small, small, stream that was barely there. It made just the smallest burblemumble along the edge of the village, sometimes disappearing altogether.

This stream, though, spoke right out loud with pride and assurance. In its burblemumble it said, as clear as you please, "Here I am! Walk in me, drink of me, share with me."

And Ham realized that he was hearing just what it was saying.

Ham shuffled to the stream. He looked left, and saw that the stream wandered off to the north, burblemumbling along through the drab forests and dusty fields. He looked to the right, and saw that the stream turned a corner after a ways, burblemumbling all the way. And Ham realized that the stream was coming from the south and going to the north. He didn't know if this meant anything. Ham had never really thought about a stream coming from and going to. Just like the well in the middle of Dusk, he always thought of streams as just being.

As Ham tasted this thought, he scratched his head, he tasted the dust and grit in his mouth, felt the scritching of grit behind his eyelids, and felt the dirt between his toes and under his fingernails. He thought about evenings in Dusk, and realized that there was neither fire nor pot here. But there was an abundance of water. And the water looked to be clear and clean and chill. With that, Ham stripped off every stitch of clothing and stepped into the stream.

No thought of modesty occurred to Ham at that moment. He was overwhelmed with the stroking and smoothing sensation of the water. At home in Dusk, the water just lay there. Here in the stream, it wove through his legs, tousled his hair, rinsed clean his eyes, and played with him as though he were an old friend.

Ham lay down, as far as he could, and looked up at the sky. He watched the drab overcast as he lay in the water, letting the stream play and pounce. He couldn't remember ever just lying still and watching the sky before. After all, in the village of Dusk in the land of Dank, no one really thought about the sky much. It was just there. But today, this afternoon, the sky was alive.

The clouds overhead moved and changed. They met, they merged, and something new was formed each time. The light, too, changed as the clouds changed. It grew brighter and dimmer as the clouds moved and merged. Ham was fascinated, and lay in the stream for a long time, while his fingers and toes puckered and shriveled.

Finally, Ham realized that he was cold. The stream, in its playfulness, had grown chill as the sun (such as it was) slowly hid below the horizon. Ham stood and dripped and took his clothes from the bank of the stream and rinsed them thoroughly, watching as first mostly mud, then mostly brown water, and finally clear water ran out of his clothes.

As Ham stood in the stream, watching the dirt and dust and grit run from his clothes, he wondered where that dirt would end up in its journey.

CHAPTER 13

The weather being not too hot and not too cold, Ham laid out his sleeping blankets by the far side of the stream, lay down on them, and spread out his clothes to dry. Never before had Ham just lay on his back and looked at the sky.

"How can this be?" Ham wondered. "How can I have spent my entire life, before this day and this time, without just lying on my back and looking at the sky? The sky was always there, and my back was always there, and the ground was always there, and yet..."

This was a difficult thought for Ham, and he didn't work at it too hard nor let it work at him too hard. It also didn't occur to Ham that maybe this was a new thought for a Huddler of Dank.

The afternoon turned into evening, and Ham and his clothes dried and he rolled up in his blankets beneath the evening sky and slept.

Ham was on the road, looking east, toward where he believed the Lightbringer to be. He was floating just a couple of inches above the ground, and seemed to be able to move effortlessly. He turned to look behind him, and all was dark and dull and he could see no hint of light or color to the west.

He turned back to the east, and could see light and a blossoming of colors awaiting him. He looked to his left, to the north, and saw that there was a glorious forest of greens and golds and reds, with delectable fruits hanging from the branches, and the ground covered in soft leaves and grass. He turned to the south, and he saw plains with green and gold grasses, flowers by the millions in all colors and shades, gently rolling hills on which deer played and ate and slept, and above which birds of all kinds swooped and screamed and swept the air.

And Ham turned back to the east, to that light and color that called him, drew him, urged him on, and he walked just above the ground toward his goal.

Ham awoke and was confused. He had a sense, a hint, of a remarkable and enchanting vision, and a sense of loss and sorrow that it was gone. Tears rolled down his cheeks, as he lay in his blankets beneath the overcast sky, and fell with gentle plops onto the blankets.

Ham shook his head, wondering and knowing at the same time. He got up, got dressed, and had a bite of bread and cheese and a few sips of water.

He turned back to face the west, toward the village of Dusk. He had come so far that all he could see was the road and the drab forest and dull fields.

He looked at the stream, just in front of him.

He turned to his left, looking to the south, and said right out loud "Welcome, stream. I hope your journey has been pleasant."

Ham looked straight ahead of him, back to the west and said: "Thank you, stream, for the gift of your flowing gentleness."

Ham looked to his right, to the north, and said "Farewell, stream. I hope your journey and mine cross again."

With that, Ham turned his face around to the east, packed up his sleeping blankets and his food bag, slung his pack and his water bag over his shoulder, and began walking.

CHAPTER 14

A few hours of walking brought Ham to the edge of another village. Another village! In all of his life, and the lives of his family and friends in Dusk, Ham had never heard of anyone who had been to – or come from – another village.

"I suppose," thought Ham, "that there have been other villages all along. Why has no one ever visited between villages?"

This was another new thought. Somehow, without being aware of it, Ham had slipped right out of his Huddler groove into a new way of thinking about the world. It all started with his dream of the Lightbringer, a dream that had become a vision that he carried with him all the time, now.

As Ham came closer to the village, he saw the Huddlers of that village glance up and then continue on their way. He had expected that maybe one of them would say hello or even show a bit of curiosity. After all, no one had ever walked between villages before!

Ham saw an older fellow walking across the center of the village, head down, eyes down, feet shuffling. Ham strode up (yes, strode up) to the man and said "Good morning."

The man barely raised his eyes, and opened his mouth just a crack. "H'lo". And on he shuffled.

Ham walked after him, and said "My name is Ham. I'm from Dusk. I'm seeking the Lightbringer. Have you seen him?"

The man didn't even raise his eyes this time. "No Lightbringer." And on he shuffled, dust puffing with each tedious step.

Ham paused and thought.

"He's not curious. He probably doesn't even know who the Lightbringer is. And he doesn't seem to care. How can I find the Lightbringer if no one will even stop to talk to me?"

Ham decided to stop each person who crossed the center of the village and ask if they knew of, or had seen, the Lightbringer.

Old women said "No Lightbringer."

Young men said "No Lightbringer."

Married couples said "No Lightbringer."

And not one said "What is a Lightbringer?" or "Who is the Lightbringer?" or "Why do you care?" or "Where are you from?"

They shuffled, they mumbled, they continued on as they had the day before and the day before that.

Around noon, Ham decided to take a break for lunch. He settled down on a tree trunk bench in the center of the village (there was a tree trunk bench and a well in the center of this village, just as there had been in Dusk), took off his traveling pack, pulled out his food wallet, and prepared himself a lunch of dull bread, boring beans, and a couple of sips of water.

As Ham ate, he watched the folk of this village ("I wonder what the name of this village is?") shuffle to and fro. Not one stopped to talk to him. Several raised their eyes just enough to see that he was there. Until...

A young man, of about Ham's age, stopped. He was walking past Ham, who was still sitting on the tree trunk bench, eating his lunch of dull bread and boring beans, when the fellow just... stopped.

"H'lo," he said.

Ham stopped chewing, sat up straight, and said "Hello!"

"New?" mumbled the fellow.

"Yes, I've just come to your village from my village of Dusk. What is the name of this village?"

"Drear."

"My name is Ham. What is your name?"

"Hal."

As you can see, this was not a very exciting conversation. Of course, Hal was a typical Huddler in most ways... most ways but one – he had seen Ham and wondered and stopped and said "H'lo."

"How'd y'get here?" asked Hal.

"I walked," said Ham "and bathed in a stream and watched the sky."

Hal seemed to consider this for a minute. He raised his head and looked at the sky. He looked toward the edge of the village where their own stream lay. And then he looked back at Ham and asked "Walked?"

CHAPTER 15

"Yup, I walked."

Hal seemed to ponder this for a bit. He scratched his head through his floppy brown hair. He kicked at the dirt with his worn but serviceable brown boots. He pulled a bit of lint from his pants pocket and dropped it. He blinked, and he looked at Ham and asked…

"Why?"

This was a major step for a Huddler – curiosity.

Ham considered his answer carefully, since he didn't want the conversation – such as it was – to end.

"When I was little, I had a dream… a vision… of a man. He was different from everyone in our village. He was taller and his hair was a different color and his eyes were a different color and he walked differently. And somehow, I heard a voice calling him 'the Lightbringer'.

"Ever since the first time, I've had that dream over and over. I never really thought much about it until just a little while ago. And then, the other day, I knew… I knew that I had to go out and find the Lightbringer. I'm not sure exactly what that means. I just know that I have to do it."

Hal looked at Ham for a while. He looked down at the tips of his boots and scuffed the dirt. He looked up at the dreary sky, and tipped his head to the left, and then to the right. He held his hands out in front of him, as though he'd never seen them before, and turned them over and then back again. He pulled a worn brown rag out of his back pocket and gave his nose a good blow, then wiped his face with the rag and put the rag back in his back pocket.

"Okay. Mebbe I can help?"

Ham was stunned. While the Huddlers huddled together for security and safety, and while they were not against helping each other, it never occurred to Ham that someone would offer to help him in his quest. At that moment, he realized that it was a quest of some sort.

Ham thought it over for the time it took two dull brown birds to fly across the center of the village and land on the roof of one of the drab houses that lined the space like silent, hunched Huddlers. The birds walked to the very edge of the roof and sat down, as if waiting to hear Ham's next words.

"Then let's get you ready to go, because I don't know how far or how long this trip will be. Let me show you what I've got, and we'll make the same things for you."

First, though, Ham decided that he needed to add something to his equipment.

Ham and Hal walked out of the center of Drear and into the nearby woods.

Ham and Hal came to a small stand of oak trees. Ham knew, from his woodcutting, that oak is strong and straight and flexible when it needs to be. They searched for some fallen branches of the right length and size, and found several that would suit them just fine. They took the branches back to the bench in the center of the village.

While they were walking, Ham would look over and find Hal just watching him. Hal would tip his head to the right and then to the left.

When they got back to the bench, Ham began stripping the bark from one of the branches he'd picked up. It was slow but satisfying work, and he found himself enjoying the rich smell of the wood, the texture of the bark and the wood beneath, and the simple pleasure of the work. In its own way, this was much like chopping wood. Using his belt knife, which was honed to a clean, sharp edge, Ham would strip a section of bark, feel the wood beneath, rotate the branch a bit, and then do it again. With each strip that came off, he felt a strange emotion that he couldn't quite put words to.

Hal watched Ham for a bit, and then began to work on a branch of his own.

"Why're we takin' off the bark?"

Ham was startled by the sound of Hal's voice. He had been in a meditative state, totally absorbed in the task of stripping the bark from the branch. He realized that he had known, without really thinking about it, that they needed to strip the bark. Now he had to think about why he was doing it so he could explain to Hal.

"We'll be walking, right?"

"Yup."

"And while we're walking, we'll be holding our sticks, right?"

"Yup."

"Well, I guess that the bark would be pretty rough on our hands, and if we take it off and smooth the sticks, it won't be so hard on our hands."

Hal got one of his looks again, tipped his head side to side, gave a short nod, and went back to stripping the bark from his branch.

When they'd removed all the bark from their branches, they used their knives to trim the ends flat, take off the little branches along the length of each branch, and smooth the wood. They did some scraping and smoothing until each staff was comfortable in their hands. Then Ham looked around.

In the center of the village was the village well, where the Huddlers of Drear came to fetch their water daily, just as in Dusk. Across from where Ham and Hal sat working on their staffs was the village smokehouse. Ham thought for a bit, then he got up and headed toward the smokehouse. Hal followed along, carrying his own staff.

When they got to the smokehouse, Ham went in and found the smoke pit with the huddled embers. Hanging from racks above the smoke pit were strips and haunches of meat. The smokehouse keeper was sitting on a small bench off to the side, where the drafts from a small window kept the worst of the smoke from his eyes.

Ham took his staff and put one end of it into the embers, twisting it around a bit until it settled in nicely. Sparks popped and flew. Hal watched, then followed Ham's example. Hal, being Hal, looked at Ham and cocked his head to one side – just one side – and waited.

Ham said "Have you ever noticed how the ends of sticks that have been in the fire are sort of black and hard?"

Hal pondered. He looked at the toes of his boots and the backs of his hands before he answered.

"Sure, I guess."

"Well, if we're going to be walking with these and putting the ends into the ground over and over, maybe they'll last longer if they're harder."

Hal's eyes opened just a little wider, and he tipped his head from side to side, and said "hunh!"

They stood quietly, watching the ends of their sticks slowly charring, sparks floating and flaring, and the smoke drifting up and caressing the hanging meat on its way to the hole in the roof. Ham felt the closeness of the smokehouse both physically and spiritually, realizing that he was aware of Hal standing beside him and a curious bond that was forming between them.

CHAPTER 16

When the sticks looked to Ham to be just right, Ham and Hal pulled them out of the fire, doused the ends in the bucket of water that the smokehouse master kept by the door, and took the sticks – now staves – outside. With their belt knives, the two young men quickly scraped away the outer layer of charred wood to reveal the black, hard knot that had been formed by the smokehouse fire pit.

Hal looked at the end of his staff, then banged it experimentally on the ground. There was a spurt and a puff of dirt and dust. Hal raised the end of his staff to examine it, and found that – other than being a bit dirty – it was still hard and smooth.

"Hunh!"

Ham looked at Hal and smiled.

"Let's get you ready for our trip, Hal," Ham said.

"'kay," said Hal, never one to waste words, as though each was a precious resource to be hoarded and spent with judicious restraint.

The two soon-to-be traveling companions moved back to the center of Drear. Having a bit more experience as a traveler now, Ham moved quickly to show Hal what needed to be done. They assembled Hal's carry pack, some food, some clothing, a blanket roll to sleep in, and then Ham showed Hal how to make a carry bag for his water. As Ham showed Hal, he noticed that some of the Huddlers of Drear would pay just the smallest, slightest, tiniest bit of attention to what they were doing, looking sideways, walking a bit crabwise, as though they didn't really want to look but felt drawn to what Ham and Hal were doing.

When Hal's kit was all assembled, and Ham could not think of anything more to be done, the two young men headed eastward out of town, the wan sun drawing them forward as it settled to the horizon, and the first signs of dusk shadowed the village. As they reached the edge of the village of Drear, Hal stopped.

"Leaving," Hal observed. He looked back over his shoulder at the village he had been born in, had grown up in, and in which he had learned everything he knew, up until now. Ham could see Hal's eyes touch the roofs of the homes and the smokehouse and the well in the center of the village.

"Yes, we're leaving. I expect we'll be back at some point. I just don't know when."

Hal cocked his head to the left and looked at Ham, then cocked his head to the right. He took a firm grip on his staff, shrugged his shoulders beneath the straps of the pack on this back, and took his first step across the unseen but very real boundary of Drear.

CHAPTER 17

At first, Hal sort of shuffled along the path that led out of Drear to the east. His eyes were aimed downward, as though his feet moving outside of the village were the most fascinating thing in the world. Ham watched, carefully not turning his head but pushing his eyes as far to the left as they would go so he could see Hal without seeming to watch.

Ham wondered what had changed for him, that he walked with his head up and his eyes forward and a feeling of walking – even striding – instead of shuffling and hiding. He had grown up in the same environment as Hal. He had had the same schooling, learned the same ways of doing things, and lived his entire life among people who moved and spoke and huddled the same as the folk of Drear. And yet...

As Ham watched Hal out of the corners of the corners of his eyes, he saw something just barely begin to change. It wasn't much, and it wasn't fast, and it wasn't all the time. But it was there –the slightest upward movement of Hal's head, so that his eyes left the ground right in front of him and saw a bit more of the world ahead. Then his head would settle back down, and his eyes would continue their journey with his feet.

They walked for a couple of hours, and Ham began to notice more and more of the world around them. The trees were still looking sad, but Ham saw that the young ones were different. The young trees seemed to have hope – reaching upward for the bits of sunlight that reached them, standing as tall as they could. It seemed to Ham that as the trees got older and taller, just like the villagers of Dusk and Drear, they began to hunch and huddle. Rather than hopeful, they seemed sad and forlorn.

"Hal?"

"mmhmm"

"Why'd you come?"

There was a quiet humming sound from Hal, accompanied by the scuffing sounds of their boots, the flitting sound of a bird hopping from one branch to another, and the soft swishing of a breeze that ruffled Ham's hair and left Hal's untouched.

"Something... important, maybe?"

As Ham strode and Hal shuffled, and the breeze swished and ruffled, Ham thought this over. His dream was important to him, of course. Why would it be important to Hal or anyone else?

"Okay. Thanks."

And out of the corner of his left eye, where he'd been keeping an eye on Hal, Ham saw Hal seem to straighten up a bit more.

Could it be hope? Pride? What is it that is making a difference to Hal? Ham wondered. And where did I get whatever it is that is making a difference to Hal? I'm just a Huddler from the village of Dusk, following a strange dream. That dream, along with my differences, has always made me feel an outsider. And now Hal is following me on my quest, and he's changing.

Of course, Ham didn't realize that even his thinking had been changing since he began his quest. While his outside differences had always been noticeable to the folks of Dusk, and while his dream had set him apart a bit, he'd never noticed any real differences on the inside. Until today.

CHAPTER 18

The sun set. The air chilled. The birds settled into the trees. It was quiet and calm in the part of Dank that held Ham and Hal.

During his visit to Drear, Ham had realized that he had no fire, nor any way to make one. At home, in Dusk, there were fire tenders and smokehouse tenders and others, whose responsibility was to make and tend fires. Ham had never had to worry about it. His worries were about making sure they had enough wood to burn in the fires and to make charcoal. So while he was in Drear, Ham had sought out the fire tender and asked him how to make and tend fires.

The fire tender had shrunk away from Ham in fear and confusion. In Drear, as in the rest of Dank, Huddlers didn't seek to learn others' skills. You learned the skills of your mother or father, and you practiced those skills all your life, and you taught them to your children, and so it went. Ham learned two new skills that day: the skill of fire tending, and the skill of gentle persuasion. It took Ham two hours to get the fire tender to show him how to use two special types of rocks to strike a spark. It took him another hour to get the fire tender to show and explain about dry wood shavings for tinder, and building a fire slowly. When Ham and Hal had left Drear, Ham carried in his carry pack one of each of the special types of rocks, and a small batch of dry wood shavings (even though he knew, now, how to make more).

As the evening chilled and stilled, Ham and Hal moved off the barely visible, barely defined path they were following. They found a small clearing within a ring of huddled trees. They gathered some stones and laid them out in a circle.

Hal helped, cocking his head first to the left, and then to the right, with each new task. As had been true with Ham, Hal had never learned to make or tend fire, nor even wondered how.

They gathered some dry fallen branches (sadly, many of the branches, falling from the dry hopeless trees, were indeed dry), and laid them out next to the ring of stones. Then Ham pulled out his special rocks and his wood shavings. He carefully placed a small pile of the smallest and driest of the wood shavings in the middle of the ring of stones. Hal watched, cocking his head left, then right.

Ham took the two special stones, leaned close to the wood shavings, and struck the stones together. There was a small "click" and a small spark and then quiet and almost-darkness. Ham tried again, and a larger spark sprung from the stones to the wood shavings. Ham leaned close and took a deep breath, puffed out his cheeks, and let a small whoo of air out from between his lips. The spark made more sparks, the sparks spread gently into the shavings, and soon there was the smallest flame dancing on the wood shavings. Ham took some of the smallest of the sticks they'd gathered, and gently fed them into the little flame until they, too, caught some of the flame and began to burn.

Finally, there was a fire dancing for joy in their circle of stones.

Hal looked over at Ham, cocked his head to the left (yes, only to the left), and said, "Ham? Never saw a carry pack before. You made one."

"Yup, I guess I did."

"And never saw a water bag for carrying water before. You made one."

"I suppose that's true, too, Hal."

"Woodworkers make wooden tools and stuff, but you aren't a woodworker and you made walking sticks."

"Yup."

"And now you made fire."

"Yup."

"Why?"

Of all the things that Ham had going through his head, the question "Why?" hadn't been there. He was thinking about his dream of the Lightbringer. He was thinking about how Hal was changing. He was thinking about how he'd left his village and found another and about Hal and why he was coming along and... Not the question "Why?"

"Y'know, Hal, I don't really know. How 'bout if I sleep on it and give it some thought, and tell you what I think in the morning?"

Hal cocked his head to the right, finishing the movement at last, and said "'kay."

CHAPTER 19

That evening set the pattern for their evening stops. After getting the fire started, they laid out their sleeping blankets, filled a pot with some water, and heated up a meal of beans and bread and a bit of fruit. By the time they finished all of these activities and settled down on their blankets near the fire, it was fully dark. They could smell the rich aroma of the wood fire as the smoke curled around them on its journey. They could hear a few birds rustling in trees as they, too, settled in for the night.

Ham lay back on his blankets and looked up at the sky. As always the sky was somewhat overcast and dim. There was a momentary break in the clouds, just enough for a couple of stars to be seen, like tiny bits of glass nestled in cotton. Ham found himself wondering about the stars. In spite of his differences and his curiosity, he had never wondered about the stars before.

"Hal?"

"Mmhmm?"

"Have you ever wondered about the stars?"

"Waddayamean?"

"Look – see them up there?"

"Yup."

"What are they doing up there?"

For a time, there was a bit of buzzing and rustling and smoke swirling while Hal considered.

"Dunno."

Ham looked at the sky and thought some more.

"Do you wonder?"

"Never have, until now."

"I think that the stars have something to do with my dreams."

Hal was quiet, once again, while he thought over what Ham had said.

"May… be."

And they went to sleep.

19–INTERLUDE–20

It is time.

Think you so?

Indeed. Are you ready?

If I must, so be it.

Then it will be.

CHAPTER 20

Ham and Hal began another day of their journey.

Ham leaned over the cooled fire that he'd made the night before. He hovered his hand over the fire pit, and found just a hint of warmth. With the greatest of care, he sprinkled dry wood shavings into the remains of the fire, and tickled them with a few breaths. The shavings caught, and Ham quickly added enough sticks to make a small fire, just as he'd learned from the fire tender in Drear.

Hal put some water in their pot, and put it over the fire to heat up.

"So?" asked Hal.

"Hmm?"

"Why?"

Ham had to think, for a minute, what Hal was talking about. His head had been filled with stars and fires and walking sticks and wonder. Then he remembered Hal's question of the night before.

"Why? Why am I doing this and learning these things?"

"Yup."

"You know about my dream – my vision – of the Lightbringer. And you know why I'm out searching."

Hal cocked his head left, looked closely at Ham, then cocked his head right.

"Yup."

"Well, I guess I feel like I had to learn these things. I mean, I couldn't take a whole village with me. But I could take some of what they know how to do with me. So each time I find something I need, instead of asking the person who knows how to do it to go with me,

I ask them to teach me. Sometimes I figure things out by myself, like the water bag."

"Hunh. A village in your head. Hunh."

Ham waited, but it seemed that Hal had used up his conversation for that morning.

Together they made some strong, aromatic tea, had a few bites of bread and cheese, and cleaned up their camp. They poured some water over the fire, rolled up their blankets, put their utensils and fire making tools into their carry packs, and turned their faces to the east again.

Facing the sun as it climbed the sky, hidden behind the usual veil of cloud, Ham asked Hal "Do you remember my question from last night about the stars?"

"Mmhmm."

"Well, here's another wonder for you. Have you ever wondered about the sun? How it goes up the sky and down the sky and then goes away at night?"

Ham knew what to expect, at this point, and he wasn't disappointed. Hal cocked his head to the left, looked at Ham, looked at the sun, looked back at Ham, cocked his head to the right and said "Nope."

At that moment, the sun shone through the clouds for the briefest of instants, lighting the land and the trees and Ham and Hal. For that moment, it seemed to Ham that he saw everything around him with startling clarity, each tree and rock and blade of grass standing out in detail against the background of earth and sky – green of plants against brown of earth, and the blue-gray of the sky against the brown-green of the horizon.

Looking toward the horizon, Ham saw a short, bent, dusty brown figure walking towards them from the east, its pale shadow extended as if to reach out and touch them. The figure carried a walking stick, although the stick, like the figure, seemed short and bent. Ham and Hal, never having seen another soul outside of their villages, stopped in stunned silence and waited.

The figure slowly shuffled toward them, its head bent, its eyes on the ground, its walking stick making a scrape-thud sound with each step. As the figure came closer, Ham could see that it was an old, old man. In fact, Ham had never seen anyone that old. The man's hair was all white, wispy, and thin on top. His shoulders were hunched and his back bent. He had a pack of sorts on his back, and was wearing some kind of cloak that hid his clothing. Ham could hear a clinking sound, but could not see what might be making the sound because of the cloak.

Finally the man reached them, and stopped. He looked up from beneath bushy white eyebrows, and his eyes flashed and took in Ham and Hal in a quick glance. Ham felt, in that instant, that the old man had learned everything about him in that one glance, and it felt strange.

"Hello, Ham. Hello, Hal. I'm Martin."

Ham was stunned. How could this man – this Martin – possibly know their names? Hal, well, Hal cocked his head to the left, then cocked it back to the right, and said "Yup" as if it was the most natural thing in the world to meet a total stranger who knew their names.

Ham managed to stammer out "You know who we are. How did you know that?"

Martin said "I've been looking for you. Well, I've been waiting for you for a long time, and just started looking for you a few weeks ago. I started out from my village, many miles from here, and just now found you. I hope you're worth it!"

CHAPTER 21

H am looked Martin up and down. This was the most startling thing he had heard. Martin didn't look crazy. Somehow he knew Ham's and Hal's names and had come looking for them. Ham hadn't known that he would be going on his journey until shortly before he set out, and certainly there was no way that someone from a distant village could know anything about it.

"Why would you be looking for me... for us?"

Martin looked up from beneath his bushy white brows, once again, and seemed to consider. His eyes were different, somehow. As Ham thought about this, he realized that Martin's eyes were blue. Ham had never seen a Huddler with blue eyes before.

Of all the oddities and strangenesses that he had encountered thus far, this might be the oddest and strangest.

He found himself staring into Martin's surprising eyes, as if he might find some answers hidden in their depths. He became so intent, so focused, that he was surprised when Martin started speaking...

"I'll answer your question with a question. Why are you out here wandering around?"

Ham didn't have to think about this. He knew why he was out wandering around. Although he wouldn't have called it "wandering around".

"I had a dream, a vision. In that dream, I saw a man – that man was different from anyone I'd ever known – taller, stronger, more confident. His eyes were a bit different, and his hair was a bit different, and the way he walked – well – it was different too.

"One day, I realized two things about this man. First, that he was called the Lightbringer. Second, I had to go find him.

"I don't know exactly how I knew, I just knew."

Martin looked at him from beneath the clouds of his brows, and smiled. "You just knew. And I just knew."

There was a moment of silence in which Ham suddenly felt... connected to Martin. He looked at Hal, and sure enough Hal's head was tilted to the left, while he looked at Martin. Then Hal looked toward Ham, and his head tilted to the right. And he gave a small, quiet smile, and said "...just knew."

The three of them stood there, with the breeze tickling their ears and the birds chirping gently in the trees, while the branches and the leaves of the trees created a sweet soothing sound.

"Martin," Ham said softly, almost as thought speaking to himself, "just knew..."

"We're heading east," said Ham, "looking for the Lightbringer. Since you seem to have found us, are you coming with us?"

Martin cackled gently, straightened his back just a bit, and said "Well, of course, young searcher. Would I come all this way only to say hello and then go home again?"

"Honestly, I don't know what you'd do," said Ham, with just a little bit of frustration slipping into his voice. "I don't know you, and don't know why you're here. I don't even really know why I'm here!"

"Young Ham, you are following a dream, a vision, maybe a message from the gods. There are few higher purposes than that."

Ham was thunderstruck by this. It had never occurred to him, until that very moment, that his dreams and visions might be messages from gods. Ham sat down in the dirt, somewhat abruptly. Hal, looking confused, sat down beside him. Martin found a rock nearby, and slowly creaked his way down onto that rock.

"Gods? A message from the gods? Could it be?"

"And why not? Who are we to say what does or does not come from the gods? All I know is that I knew I had to find you, I knew your names as soon as I saw you, and I know that I'm supposed to travel with you while you search for the Lightbringer. I can wonder and worry about where that knowing comes from, or I can follow where it leads me. I'm old, I've lived a full if somewhat boring life, and I'm ready and willing to follow along.

"Is that okay with you, Young Ham?"

Ham just sat and stared and stared and sat. This was so far outside of what he had ever known that he didn't even know where to begin.

Gods and knowing and journeying. Just ten days ago, this would never even have occurred to him. And yet, here he was, with Hal –

whom he had just met and who kept cocking his head from side to side like a curious bird – and Martin, the oldest man he'd ever seen, who said the queerest things as if to say "isn't it a nice day?"

And he still felt like he was just Ham, the woodchopper, from Dusk.

CHAPTER 22

H am sat for a moment longer. He looked up at Hal and Martin, and saw that both of them were grinning slightly. With some embarrassment, Ham stood up and dusted himself off, particularly the seat of his pants.

"Well," Ham pronounced, "let's be on our way then. I see that you have a travel pack, too, Martin. So unless there's something you need here and now, let's be off!"

Martin smirked a bit, winked slyly at Hal, and gestured for Ham to lead the way. Hal fell back to walk alongside Martin, both of them trailing Ham. "Just knew, hmm?"

"Yes, young Hal, I just knew. Just as I know that you aren't nearly as dense and slow as you'd have everyone think."

Hal cocked his head to the left, considered Martin for a moment, cocked his head to the right, considered Martin a bit more, then bringing his head center and forward-facing again, he said "mmmm."

For the first hour or so, Ham walked in the lead, not speaking to either Hal or Martin. They could see that his shoulders and neck were stiff, and that he made an effort not to turn his head and look at them. They could see the strain this was causing in the tight wiry muscles along his neck, and each, separately, wondered when he would let it go.

As they climbed a short hill, Ham slowed down a bit until Hal and Martin caught up with him. He looked at Hal on his left, then turned and looked at Martin on his right. He sighed, then smiled slightly, and kept walking over the crest of the hill.

CHAPTER 23

This set the pattern for several days of traveling, during which they saw only each other. There were no villages and no other huddlers. There were birds and deer and other animals. There were brooks and rocks and trees and they even found a cave one evening.

No villages. No Huddlers.

During this time, they walked and they talked.

In spite of his age and the curve of his back and shoulders, Martin seemed to have no difficulty keeping up with the younger men. Sometimes, while climbing a hill, Martin would huff a bit when he reached the top. Regardless, he neither complained nor grumbled.

Their talk rambled far more than they did. While their walking took them steadily eastward, their talk ran all over the landscape.

A lot of their talk dealt with why's and how's. Why did Ham set out? How did he make the water bag? Why did he learn to make fire? How did he expect to find the Lightbringer? Why did Hal join him?

The questions started to repeat, although the answers grew with each exchange.

Ham still didn't know exactly what had led him to leave the well-known security of his village. He still didn't know where or how he would find the Lightbringer. He didn't know exactly why Hal had joined him nor why Martin was sent to them (and he was sure, after several days of conversation, that Martin was sent).

He did know that he would – must – complete his quest to find the Lightbringer.

CHAPTER 24

The three travelers came upon another village late on the afternoon of the fourth day after Martin arrived. It was laid out just like the villages of Dusk and Drear: a well in the center, a small stream running along the side of the village, and the huts and homes built around the center of the village.

The travelers walked slowly into the center of the village. There were some cut logs lying along the side, clearly there for the villagers to sit on. Ham and Hal and Martin went to the logs and sat.

The villagers, typical of Huddlers, shuffled on their errands, heads down, with that slightly fearful look on their faces at all times. Some would glance quickly under their lashes and brows at the strangers sitting on their logs in the center of their village.

One young woman shuffled up to them as they sat, quietly, absorbing the village.

"Strangers?"

"Yes," said Ham.

"We are," said Martin.

"mmmm," said Hal.

"My name is Rachel," the young woman said.

Hal cocked his head to the left, looked her in the eye, cocked his head to the right, gave a small smile, brought his head to the center and said "Hal."

Ham and Martin exchanged a brief look, Ham's eyes opening just a bit wider than usual. Martin nodded as if to agree with something.

"We've just come to your village. I'm searching for the man known as the 'Lightbringer'. Have you heard of him?" asked Ham.

Rachel looked at the dirt at her feet, shuffled her feet forward and back a bit, hunched her left shoulder, then her right, and said "… don't think so."

Hal grinned again.

Ham said "Oh, well. What is the name of this village, Rachel?"

Rachel looked at Ham, her eyes a bit wide. It seemed clear that she was surprised that someone wouldn't know the name of her village.

"Wait."

Ham waited for a minute, during which there was the sound of a slight breeze blowing across the roofs of the huts and homes in the village. When Rachel didn't say anything further, Ham asked again, "What is the name of this village, Rachel?"

"Wait."

Again Ham waited. Had Ham looked to his left, he would have seen Martin's small, satisfied smile.

After another minute, Ham asked "What are we waiting for, Rachel?"

Rachel looked confused. She hunched her left shoulder, hunched her right shoulder, and said "Nothing."

Now it was Ham's turn to look confused. He looked at Martin on his left, and saw that Martin was smiling. He looked to his right, and saw that Hal had his head cocked to the left.

Hal cocked his head to the right, smiled at Ham, brought his head to the center, and said "…name is Wait."

Ham paused for a moment, and then started laughing. He laughed himself right off the log, and onto the ground. He laughed so hard, tears cleared a path through the dirt on his cheeks. He laughed so hard, his belly hurt and he had trouble catching his breath.

While Ham laughed, Hal cocked, Rachel hunched, and Martin smiled.

"Wait," Ham gasped, "the name is Wait!"

And off he went into more laughter.

Other Huddlers from the village of Wait began to gather. In all of their lives, none had ever seen someone laugh like this. Most looked confused, while a few looked afraid.

Finally Ham stopped laughing, picked himself up from his bath of dirt, brushed himself off – as well as he could – and sat back down on his log.

"Wait," he said, with a grin.

"May we stay here tonight?" Ham asked, to no one in particular.

Villagers looked from one to the other, huddling, shuffling, and shrugging. Finally Rachel said "there is an empty house on the north side. The people who lived there died some time ago, and they had no children, and there have been no other folks who needed a home. So it might not be clean, but it's empty, and you can stay there."

Ham just stared. This was the longest speech he'd ever heard from another Huddler, except for Martin. Hal smiled, cocked his head back and forth, and said "…thanks."

"I'll show you."

Rachel led them to the north side of the village. There was a small, browngray structure somewhere between a hut and a house. There was a leather curtain for a door, a hole in the roof for smoke to get out, two windows with rickety shutters, and a yard that was all dirt.

Ham walked into the hut and looked around. There was a cot on one side of the big room, a couple of roughly made chairs, and a fireplace under the hole in the roof.

"Thank you, Rachel. This will do just fine."

The three travelers took off their carry packs.

There was no wood or scrap in the hut, so Ham went off in search of some wood to make a fire. As he strolled through the village, he noticed the Huddlers of Wait looking at him almost expectantly. He didn't know why, and saved the question for later consideration.

When Ham got back to the hut, he saw that Hal had taken his cooking pot and gotten some water from the village well. Martin had dusted off the cot and the chairs, and was quietly sitting on the cot, looking at Hal and Rachel, who sat in the chairs.

It was an odd tableau. Four relative strangers sitting in companionable silence.

Ham cleaned the fireplace, laid in some wood shavings, and proceeded to strike his firestarters.

"Oh, you're a firemaker!"

"No, I'm a woodcutter. I learned to make fire from the firemaker in a village we passed."

Then Rachel saw the walking sticks that all three carried. "Then is one of you a woodcarver?"

"No, not really. I figured I'd need a walking stick, so I learned how to carve them from the branches of trees."

While he was talking, Ham poured some water from his water bag over his hands to clean them.

"And where did that bag come from? Do you have someone who makes those in your village?

"Um – no – I made that, too. When I decided to go on this journey, I knew I'd need water to drink. So I figured out how to make a bag to carry water in, since there wouldn't be a well around all the time."

Rachel looked a bit stunned. "You make fire, you carve sticks, and you make water bags. But no one does all those things. Firemakers make fire, carvers carve tools and implements, and bag makers make bags. How can you do all of those things?"

Martin, with a grin, asked "Yes, Ham, how?"

"Well…" at which point Ham proceeded to tell Rachel of his dream, his vision, his quest, and the journey thus far.

Rachel sat openmouthed through most of the telling. She never interrupted. Once or twice she hunched her left shoulder, then her right, and Hal would smile.

CHAPTER 25

When Ham was done with his story, Rachel asked "Will you teach me to make fire?"

Before Ham could answer, Hal stood and said "I will."

Ham caught his breath, then smiled and took the chair that Hal vacated. Hal reached out his hand to Rachel and said "...need some special rocks."

Rachel looked at Hal, took his hand, got up, and walked with Hal out into the village.

"Do you think...?" asked Ham.

"Yup," said Martin with his grin growing.

CHAPTER 26

Hal and Rachel returned some time later.

"…taught her to make fire," said Hal.

Rachel smiled shyly, shuffled her feet a bit, and leaned into Hal. Ham noticed that they were holding hands. He looked at Martin, who shrugged as if to say "you never know, do you?"

"Will you teach me how to make water bags and carve walking sticks and…?" Rachel asked, so quietly that it might have been the breeze blowing through the gaps in the walls.

Ham looked at Hal. Hal cocked his head left, then right. When his head came back to center, Hal said "…stay and teach?"

Ham was stunned to silence. He hadn't thought about Hal staying. Well, really, he hadn't thought much about Hal going or staying or what Hal's role in his journey was. So he thought about it.

He realized that Hal had his own journey. While Ham didn't know what that journey was, he did realize that Hal had come with him because Ham had appeared at the right time for Hal.

Ham said "Of course, Hal, if that's what you want."

Rachel hunched her right shoulder, then her left, beaming all the time. Hal cocked his head left, then right, then center and smiled at Rachel.

"Maybe I can stay in this house."

"I don't see why not," Rachel smiled.

And the decision was made.

Rachel left them for the night, and Ham and Hal and Martin sat in what was to be Hal's home.

"Are you sure?" Ham asked Hal.

"Why are you asking him that?" asked Martin. "Don't you think he can make up his own mind?"

"Well, sure. I just didn't really know why Hal came with me, where he wanted to go, or what he was going to do. Now that he's said he's not coming along, I kind of know that I liked having him along. But if he wants to stay in Wait with Rachel, and teach the folks here the things he's learned so far, I guess that's fine with me!"

Martin, with a sparkle in his eye, cocked his head left, cocked his head right, brought his head back to the center, shrugged his right shoulder, shrugged his left shoulder, and said "Well, now, I guess you'll just have to do with a strange old man like me!"

Ham, for no reason that he could figure out, found this unbearably funny and started laughing for the second time that day. He laughed and howled and groaned and laughed some more. He fell out of his chair, and rolled on the floor, howling with laughter the whole time.

When he was done, he lifted himself back into the chair, took a deep breath, and said "then that's the way it will be."

They sat by the fire for a time, sharing a word and a thought now and then. When the fire had settled down for the night, so did the three companions.

CHAPTER 27

"...staying for a few days?"

Hal continued to be a man of few words, but no one ever seemed to misunderstand him.

Ham and Martin hadn't had a chance to talk about their plans, such as they were. Ham looked at Hal, looked at Martin, and said "Why not?"

"Not a reason I can think of, youngster," said Martin.

And so it was that Ham and Martin chose to stay in the village of Wait for a few days, enjoying a roof over their heads and a bed they could take turns sleeping in. During the days, Ham would wander through the village, meeting some of the Huddlers there (when he could get them to look up and speak to him). Ham particularly paid attention to how each of the Huddlers performed their tasks, and made an effort to learn something of several different skills. Martin spent most of his days sitting on the logs by the well in the center of the village, watching the folk of Wait shuffling to and fro.

In the evenings, Ham and Martin talked about what they would do next, where they would go. Hal would come around for a bit, every evening, and just sit and listen. Then he would get up quietly and go off to be with Rachel.

On the third day of their stay in Wait, Hal caught up with Ham where Ham was watching the hut-builder. Hal had another young man with him.

"...Walt," said Hal. "...wants to go with you."

Ham, taken aback for a moment, looked Walt up and down. "You want to go with us?"

"Yup. Hal showed what he learned, and told about places, and I want to go."

Ham's first reaction was to go talk it over with Martin. Then he realized that he was traveling on his own quest, and didn't really need to talk about it. Then he thought oh, why not.

"Okay – come to our hut this evening and talk to me and Martin."

"How about my sister, June?"

"What do you mean, how about your sister?"

"Can she come too? Wants to."

A girl traveling with them? Well, why not – it's not like they had run into wild animals or bands of roving bandits.

"Bring her tonight, too."

Ham felt a bit distracted for the rest of the day. He'd never planned on Hal joining him, and it had just happened. Now Hal was sharing what he'd learned and done, and others wanted to join him. He didn't know if that meant anything, but it felt... important.

And, of course, there was Martin. Old, odd, mysterious Martin, who had come looking for them. Ham wondered why Martin was there, and what he expected to happen.

That evening, while Ham and Martin sat by the fire in Hal's soon-to-be hut, Hal and Walt and June arrived. Ham explained to Martin that Walt and June wanted to travel with them, and that he – Ham – couldn't think of any reason why they shouldn't.

"Young folks, why do you want to go with Ham?"

"Learn and see," said Walt.

"Be more, do more," said June.

Martin smiled one of his strange, knowing smiles, and looked at Ham. He shrugged his shoulders, as if to say "I don't see why not."

Ham thought about staying in Wait for a few days, as if they'd been – well – waiting for something. Maybe they'd been waiting for Walt and June?

"Okay – you can come with us. We'll leave day after tomorrow. Tomorrow you have to get together the things you'll need on the journey. Hal can show you what to do, right Hal?"

"…mmhmm…"

CHAPTER 28

That night, Ham had a new dream about the Lightbringer. In the dream, Ham saw the Lightbringer coming toward him. That was pretty much the same as before. But this time, he saw that there were people coming along behind the Lightbringer!

When Ham woke up in the morning, he was smiling. He didn't know quite why, but he felt good. As he splashed some cool water over his face and dressed, the good feeling continued. It was like a small warm glow in his body, like every ache and discomfort was gone and everything felt just right.

Throughout the day, Ham found himself smiling for no reason. Not big, huge, joy-eating smiles; just small, savoring, happy smiles. Of course, the people of Wait walked wide around him, since the smiles made them nervous.

Several times during the day, Ham found Hal and Walt and June making preparations. Sometimes Rachel was with them. It seemed like when Rachel was with Hal, she leaned toward him. It wasn't so much something you could see, so much as something you could feel. Like her energy was more on the side where Hal was.

Walt and June were carrying sacks and packs, and seemed to be getting things done. A couple of times, they asked Ham for help, or asked him to explain something that Hal could do but not explain. By the end of the day, Walt and June said they were ready. Ham went through their sacks and packs, and he, too, said they were ready.

The new group – Ham, Martin, Walt, and June – were ready to set out the next morning. That evening, Hal and Walt and June came to visit with Ham and Martin. It was a bit too snug in the hut, so the group sat outside, under the murky sky, and talked. Rachel joined them after a bit, and sat close by Hal.

CHAPTER 29

They sat in companionable silence for a time. Rachel sat close to Hal, shoulders touching. Ham noticed that Rachel was carrying a staff in one hand, and was pretty sure that it was new. Hal cocked his head to the left, looked at Ham, smiled briefly, cocked his head to the right, looked at Rachel, and smiled again before bringing his head to the center.

Walt looked at Ham and said "I don't know for sure why you're here, even though you've told us your story. I mean, sure I understand that you're looking for the Lightbringer, but why here? Why Wait?"

"I really don't know," said Ham. "Each step of this journey has been as much a mystery to me as it is to you. I never really decided to learn the things I've learned. It just seemed the right thing to do at the time. Just like meeting Hal and having him come along just seemed right. I just know that I've got to keep going. And if I learn new things and meet new people along the way, maybe that's part of the journey's purpose."

Martin smiled his knowing smile and leaned back a bit, as if satisfied with something.

Hal said "...learned lots, now I'm sharing."

And they sat on, in companionable silence.

CHAPTER 30

The morning came, the travelers met at the center of the village, and Hal and Rachel joined them.

Hal cocked his head to the left, looked at Ham, cocked his head to the right, said "...thanks" and, smiling sadly, brought his head back to the center.

Rachel, in her now-usual position leaning against Hal, shrugged her right shoulder, shrugged her left shoulder, and said "…me, too."

Much to Ham's surprise, Hal and Rachel came and hugged him. And Hal handed him a new walking stick. This stick, unlike Ham's own roughly-carved one, was smoother and had some pictures carved along its length. As Ham looked closely, he realized that the rough pictures were of him and Hal and Martin walking down the road!

With a sniff and a tear, Ham said "Thanks, Hal."

With that, Ham and Martin and Walt and June set off through the far side of Wait.

CHAPTER 31

For the first couple of days, the small group found the traveling to be pretty much the same as what Ham and Martin had found before. Much of it was new to Walt and June, but quickly they adjusted to being outside their village of Wait and to seeing new things. They all slept under the stars in their sleeping rolls, made fires in the evening, gasped at the beauty and wonder of the stars (when they could see them), bathed in streams, and enjoyed the activity of walking and talking.

On the third day, something entirely new and strange and frightening happened.

For the first time, they met some Huddlers outside of a village!

This was strange for so many reasons. After many days of traveling alone and with others, Ham had never before met any Huddlers outside of a village. All of the Huddlers he had met had been too fearful to leave their homes, except for Hal and Walt and June. And since he was the first Huddler he'd ever met who could do the many things and make the many objects he needed for traveling, this wasn't at all surprising.

Meeting Huddlers outside of a village was surprising.

"Hello!" said Ham, waving his stick back and forth in greeting.

The Huddlers up ahead seemed to hunch together and move a few steps forward, towards Ham and his friends.

"Hello!" said Ham again, taking a step forward and smiling a bit tentatively.

The Huddlers up ahead started to separate, and moving forward, sort of moved around Ham and Martin and Walt and June. Ham looked to his left, and saw that Martin looked thoughtful. He looked to his right, and saw that Walt and June were edging towards him. He looked around, and saw that there were six of the other Huddlers in a half-circle from his left to his right.

The other Huddlers had empty hands, were extremely dirty, were hunched and tense, and were sort of leaning toward Ham and his friends.

"Hello?" Ham said, inviting, asking, testing...

CHAPTER 32

The other Huddler standing almost directly in front of Ham, maybe two paces away, said "We're hungry. Give us food."

This caught Ham completely by surprise. After all, there was food all around – hanging from trees, growing in the ground. In fact, not ten paces from where they stood was an apple tree, with ripe apples hanging.

Ham said "There are apples on that tree right there."

"We don't know how to get apples. Give us food." said the Huddler who was, apparently, the "leader" of this group.

"You just pick them," said Ham.

"We're hungry. Give us food." And the leader and the other Huddlers took a small, shuffling step forward.

For the first time in quite a while, Ham began to feel afraid. Why couldn't these Huddlers feed themselves?

"Ham?" asked June. "How did you learn about apples and trees?" in a small, frightened voice.

Ham thought. He remembered his life in his village of Dusk. There was one person there who was an apple gatherer, and another who was a water carrier, and another who was a potato grower. In fact, before he decided to leave Dusk, Ham never thought about apple trees and picking apples!

Ham realized he had a choice at this moment. He could deal with the other Huddlers trying to take their food – for that's what it felt like right then and there – or he could try to teach them how to feed themselves. And he wondered how they had managed to feed themselves thus far, if they didn't know how to pick apples from a tree right in front of them.

Ham looked at Martin and Walt and June and said "Let's feed them."

CHAPTER 33

A fter pulling some of their food out of their packs to share with the other Huddlers, Ham said to the leader, "Follow me."

Ham led the other Huddler to the apple tree, and showed him how to pick an apple. With apparent fear and unease, the other Huddler reached up and pulled loosed a rich, ripe apple. Ham bit into his own apple, and the other Huddler did the same. With the first bite, the other Huddler's eyebrows rose a bit, a small smile showed at the corners of his mouth, and he ate the whole apple in a rush.

After finishing his own apple, Ham asked "What's your name?"

"Lyle," said the other Huddler.

"And where do you come from, Lyle?" asked Ham.

"Lost," said Lyle.

After his experience with the village of Wait, Ham asked "Your village is named Lost?"

"Yup," said Lyle.

"And are those other people with you all from Lost?"

"Yup," said Lyle. "Lorna, Link, Larry, Lonny, and Lynn."

As they were asking and answering, Ham led Lyle back toward the others. He found the whole group sitting quietly, eating and watching each other.

"Lyle," said Ham, "why don't you show your friends how to pick apples?"

Lyle looked confused, for a minute. "Apple pickers pick apples."

"Yes," said Ham. "I guess now you're an apple picker."

Lyle considered, looked around the group sitting in the dirt, and gave a small smile. "Apple pickers."

With that, he led Lorna, Link, Larry, Lonny, and Lynn to the apple tree, and Ham and Martin and Walt and June could see him showing the others how to pick apples. They could hear muttering and mumbling and chewing sounds from where they sat.

When the group of Huddlers from Lost returned, Ham asked "What did you do in Lost?"

"Woodcutter," said Lyle.

"Water carrier," said Lorna.

"Tool maker," said Link.

"Fire maker," said Larry.

"House builder," said Lonny.

"Clothing maker," said Lynn.

Ham looked at them in silence for a time. He realized that none of them knew anything about growing, gathering, or preparing food. Somehow, they had left Lost, and had no idea how to survive.

And then he looked at his traveling companions and realized how much each of them had learned, and how much each of them could teach.

Ham made a decision. He decided that they would spend several days right where they were, with no villages in sight, with a small stream meandering nearby and a tree full of rich, ripe apples to eat. He and his companions would teach these six Huddlers how to do things that only others had ever done. He would help them to teach each other, as well, since each could learn the others' skills.

First, he gathered his traveling companions and explained what he intended. Each responded in his or her own unique way, each agreeing.

Ham then turned to the six Huddlers from Lost, and told them what he intended.

Lyle looked as if the sky had fallen on his head.

Lorna started crying.

Link turned around and faced the other way, sitting with his knees drawn up and his arms wrapped around his knees.

Larry just stared at Ham.

Lonny said "Why?"

Lynn said "Okay."

And Ham began. "You've already learned how to be an apple picker. Had any of you ever been an apple picker before?"

They looked at each other, shook their heads, and sat silently. Except for Link, who was still looking the other way.

"Walt and June were just like you. They did what they learned from their parents and nothing else. Until they decided to travel with me. Then they learned to make walking stick and water bags and prepare food and more."

The six from Lost looked at each other again (even Link this time, who turned around). They still looked scared. They still looked confused. But they looked and listened.

CHAPTER 34

For the next three days, Ham and Walt and June and even Martin taught the six from Lost how to survive on their own. More importantly, though, they taught them how to learn.

When they were done, Lyle asked "Can I go with you?"

Lorna, Larry, and Lynn each said "Me, too?"

Link and Lonny said "We're going back to Lost."

And so Ham's group grew from four to eight, while the things they'd shared made their way back to the village of Lost.

CHAPTER 35

Over the next months, this became a pattern.

Ham and his friends would reach another village. Ham would ask about the Lightbringer. With no luck.

Some of the group would elect to stay in the village, and some from the village would elect to travel with Ham and his group.

Martin remained a constant. Ham found that when he was feeling stumped – when he just couldn't figure out what to do – Martin would somehow have the right questions or suggestions to get him over the hump. Ham came to depend on Martin for his knowledge, his knowing smiles, and his constant guidance.

CHAPTER 36

One morning, waking in his sleeping roll with his current group of fellow travelers, Ham looked around and realized that Martin was gone.

He asked the others, but none had seen or heard a thing.

Ham went to where Martin had been sleeping, and found a small stone with a small image carved into its face. Other than that image, the stone was completely smooth, and slightly smaller than the palm of his hand. Looking carefully, Ham could see that the image was a small flame, dancing and swaying. While it was not really dancing and swaying, there was something about it that gave him the feeling of its being alive in a fire kind of way.

Ham didn't say anything to any of the others. He just put the stone in his pouch. And from time to time, as he traveled through the land of Dank, he would reach into his pouch and hold and feel the stone that was all he had of Martin.

CHAPTER 37

A day came when Ham realized it had been a long time and he had not found one hint, one whisper, one clue about the Lightbringer. He felt sad and disappointed and frustrated. He had traveled farther and wider than anyone he'd ever heard of, he still had his dreams and his vision, and he had not found what he sought.

This realization happened as Ham and his friends were sitting on the logs in the center of a village near the well. It could have been any of the villages he'd visited during his travels.

Ham's current traveling companions were Hope and Rob and Bess and Fred. Each had come from a different village along the way, and had been with him for varying lengths of time. Each seemed transformed from the people he'd originally met, standing straighter, being clearer of eye, and speaking in whole, clear sentences.

Ham looked at each of them and smiled. He might not have found the Lightbringer, but he had made many friends, learned many things, and traveled a great distance, seeing many new and different things.

It was time to go home.

Ham thought of his family: his father Horace, his mother Hannah, and his sister Helen. He didn't know exactly how long he'd been gone, but he knew it had been quite a while, and wondered how Helen had grown.

He thought about Hyram, the mayor of Dusk, and the Huddlers who were all he'd known before he set out on his quest.

It was time to go home.

Ham told Hope and Rob and Bess and Fred that he was going home, and that they were welcome to travel with him.

As had happened many times before, some chose to stay and some chose to go with him. This time, it was Hope and Rob who were going with him, and Bess and Fred who were staying.

CHAPTER 38

Setting out the next morning, Ham decided to retrace his steps so that he could see the Huddlers he had known and traveled with. And, admittedly, with the faint hope that he'd find Martin somewhere along the way.

They got back to their last village, Ford, where he'd met Fred. Things seemed pretty much the same, although there did seem to be a few new things in the village. It had only been a matter of some days – perhaps ten – so on the one hand it was not surprising and on the other hand Ham was surprised to find any changes at all.

At the next village, things were a bit more different than they had been, and he heard a few Huddlers whisper "Lightbringer". He assumed it was because they remembered that he was searching for the Lightbringer, and gave it no more thought.

CHAPTER 39

It must have been at the fourth or fifth village they came to on their way back that something noteworthy occurred.

Ham and his companions entered the village and headed for the center, as they always did, to sit by the well and relax. As they sat, one of Ham's former traveling companions, Jeff, came toward him and said "Welcome back, Lightbringer!"

Ham was, to say the least, startled and surprised.

He looked around, hoping for a glimpse of the Lightbringer. He was disappointed. All he saw were his traveling companions, Jeff, and a few Huddlers who were standing nearby and staring at him.

"Where is the Lightbringer, Jeff?"

"Where? Why standing right in front of me, of course!"

And Ham realized that Jeff was calling him Lightbringer!

"But I'm not the Lightbringer! I'm searching for the Lightbringer. I haven't found him, so I'm heading back home again."

"When you left, we talked to the other Huddlers in this village. We told them about your quest and your vision and all that you had taught us. We began to teach them some of the ways of doing things, and the ways of thinking that you taught us. They said that *you* must be the Lightbringer. Over time, they've begun referring to you as the Lightbringer, and we just went along with them."

Ham sat in stunned thought. How could they mistake him for the Lightbringer? Impossible!

And yet…

CHAPTER 40

This continued in village after village - "Welcome back, Lightbringer!" - until Ham and his companions came to a village named Rise. As always, they went to the center of the village to sit on the logs by the well.

But there were no logs. Instead, there were benches and small tables. And the ground was well cleared, and there was a clean shelf by the well with some cups on it.

As Ham and his companions sat on the logs, one of the Huddlers of Rise came to them and said "Welcome to Rise. Let me go fetch one of the Lamplighters for you."

Ham was dumbfounded, and just sat staring.

In a short while, one of his former traveling companions, Rod, came to greet him.

"Why did that Huddler call you a Lamplighter?"

Rod chuckled, and said "Will you wait until evening, so we can gather and explain to you?"

Ham, with a bit of frustration, nodded his agreement. With that, Rod went off to gather the others, and Ham and his companions sat in silence on the benches by the well, drinking the fresh well water and munching on fresh apples that one of the Huddlers of Rise brought to them.

Rod returned. "May I show you to a place where you can rest until evening?"

With Ham's assent, Rod led the small group to a house. Not a hut. Not a shack. A house. It had a door on simple hinges. It had shutters over the window openings. It had wooden floors and a fireplace and a chimney. And it had two separate rooms, each with a bed in it.

Ham was unable to speak. He stomped on the floor, listening to the sound of the wood booming and creaking. He opened and closed the doors and shutters. And he went and lay on one of the beds. It was the most comfortable bed he'd ever been on in his life. Ham was astonished. It had not been all that long since he'd been in Rise, and yet the changes were unbelievable.

CHAPTER 41

As the sun set, Rod came back to the house, knocked on the door, and invited Ham and his companions to join him in the center of the village.

The first thing that Ham noticed as he left the house was the light. There were lamps on posts at intervals around the village. Instead of stumbling around in the dark, on his way back to the center of the village, Ham could see pretty clearly where he was going. He looked over at Rod, who just grinned at him.

As they reached the center of the village, Ham found that there were lights spaced all around the center, and some more around the well, and that the space was crowded with Huddlers. As Ham arrived, there was a hush, then a rustling of movement and the sound of voices whispering "the Lightbringer". Ham looked around, still thinking that they must be talking about the man in his dream, the Lightbringer of his quest.

Rod began.

"Ham, when you came to my village some time back, you taught some of us to do things that only others had done until then. You taught us to make travel packs and sleeping rolls and prepare food for traveling and make walking sticks and more. You taught us to make bags to carry water. You taught us that it was possible to do many things, not just the things we had been taught growing up. You taught us without thinking about what it might mean, and you taught us without reservations.

"A few of us decided to stay here in Rise when you continued on your quest for the Lightbringer. We wondered, when you left, how marvelous the Lightbringer must be. After all, given all that you had taught us and all the things you've done that no one else has ever done, we thought you were pretty marvelous yourself. As time went on, we realized that as far as we were concerned, you *were* the Lightbringer, because you had brought so much that is new and wonderful into our lives, particularly in teaching us how to think about things.

"Not long after you left, for instance, we wondered about why we were stumbling around in the dark night after night. We had been teaching the Huddlers of Rise how to do many things, and at that point many knew how to make fire, and how to carry fire with them. And so we created the lamps you see around the village. It wasn't a giant step for us anymore, although it would have been before you brought the light into our lives. When we did that, the Huddlers of Rise started calling us the *Lamplighters*. We realized that it meant more than just creating and lighting lamps around the village. It also meant that we had shared the light of thinking and doing that you had brought to us.

"And so the Huddlers of Rise call us the Lamplighters, because we spread the light that you – the Lightbringer – brought to us."

Ham was, once again, speechless.

CHAPTER 42

"After a while," Rod continued, "we decided to send messengers to the villages nearby. We thought that with all you had taught us, and what we had taught the villagers of Rise, we should continue to share. So the messengers we sent were told to teach as much as they could, including the making and lighting of the lamps in the village. Of course, they also told the tale of the Lightbringer. Each of those messengers has, in turn, come to be called a Lamplighter.

"Meanwhile, here in Rise, we found that there were others who quickly (or even not-so-quickly) embraced the things we were teaching. As they embraced them, they taught others and made changes of their own. Just as the Huddlers in Rise and elsewhere came to call those of us who had learned directly from you – the Lightbringer – Lamplighters, so the other Huddlers came to call those who learned from us and spread the ideas the *Shadowpushers*, since they continued to push back the shadows and spread the light.

"No one Huddler seemed to be responsible for this. It just seemed to happen. And as the Huddlers at each of the other villages spread the learning, so they also spread the names, and now at any village nearby you will find that they know of the Lightbringer, and either have Lamplighters of their own, or Shadowpushers who learned from the Lamplighters.

"One way and another, the things you've taught us – not just the making and doing, but the thinking – have spread from village to village."

And Ham cried. And Ham laughed.

CHAPTER 43

The journey continued, and in each village they came to, Ham found more Lamplighters and Shadowpushers. He was hailed as the Lightbringer, and found himself accepting the name, even embracing it.

The physical changes in the villages grew, with each village he came to. And each time he asked about the changes, the Lamplighters and Shadowpushers explained to him that after a while, the changes just seemed to be the natural next steps from what he'd taught them originally.

Finally, Ham returned to Dusk.

It was not the Dusk he'd left.

First, there was a clear road between Drear and Dusk. Not just the hint of a path that he'd walked when he left, but a road – hard-beaten, clear edged, and well-used.

As Ham approached the village of Dusk, he saw that there was a fence. Not a gate or a fence to keep people out, just a sort of boundary around Dusk. And where the road pierced that boundary, there was an arch. The arch was made of well-cut and smoothed wood, and it had words carved on it. As Ham got closer, he saw what the words said:

Welcome to Dusk, the Home of the Lightbringer.

Bring light or take light.

Ham stood still in the middle of the road. After this long, he was no longer uncomfortable at being called the Lightbringer. But this was different.

He was home.

And home was, seemingly, proud of him.

As he walked through the arch, his family came running to greet him.

"Messengers came from Drear, telling us that you were on your way. We're so proud of you! Who knew, when you told us of your dream, that you were the Lightbringer!"

There were so many differences that Ham nearly stumbled as he walked. First was the fact that his family, who had prevously been so typical of Huddlers, were lively and vital and excited.

And then he realized that the rest of the village was much the same – lively, vital, and excited.

He saw the kinds of physical changes he'd seen elsewhere, which surprised him. After all, when he left, there were no Lamplighters to be left behind. There was no one with whom he'd shared his learning or experience.

CHAPTER 44

That evening, he sat in his family's home – much changed from the home he'd left – sharing glasses of fresh spring water, enjoying the company of Hank, the dog, and his family told him their story.

"After you left, life went on as it always had," his father Horace told him. "I continued to cut wood, your mother continued to make clothes and take care of the house, and Helen continued to go to school. Hyram continued to be Mayor, doing it the way he'd always done it, and that was that.

"Until one day, several weeks after you left, a young man came to the village. He told us that his name was Hal, and that he'd spent some time traveling with you, after you met in his village of Drear. He said that he met his wife, Rachel, while traveling with you. He said that they spent some time in Rachel's village of Wait, and then felt that they had to share what they'd learned.

"According to Hal, they visited the villages around Wait, teaching others the things you'd taught them. After a while, they met another Huddler who was also traveling to other villages, who told them that those who were sharing what they learned were being called Lamplighters, and that you were being referred to as the Lightbringer. (You can imagine our surprise on hearing this!) And he taught them how to make lamps for the village, and other things that the Lamplighters were spreading.

"Hal and Rachel decided--once they'd learned about the lamps and the Lamplighters and you as the Lightbringer--that they needed to travel to Drear and then to Dusk, as the first places you'd been.

"In Drear, as in Dusk, not much was different. Hal and Rachel began to teach and to spread the teaching. While they were there, they were surprised to have another Lamplighter visit the village. It seems, they said, that Lamplighters had taken it upon themselves to travel about the land of Dank and share your teachings. And that in each place that they went, others embraced the learning and adopted the calling of Shadowpushers. So some villages had been visited by Lamplighters – those who had traveled and learned with you – and others by Shadowpushers.

"After spending some time in Drear, Hal and Rachel came to Dusk."

At this, Horace paused and Ham looked up to see Hal and Rachel standing in the doorway of his family's home.

Hal cocked his head to the left, smiled, cocked his head to the right, winked, and then looked straight at Ham and said "Welcome home, Lightbringer!"

Rachel shrugged her right shoulder, shrugged her left, and said "We've missed you, and have done our best to share what you taught us."

And while Ham sat there tongue-tied and emotion-bound, Hank put his paws on Ham's chest, gave his cheek a big sloppy lick, and then curled up on the ground next to Ham.

************** THE END ***************

or the beginning?

Afterword:
What's the Message?

Different readers have told me that they saw different things in this book.

Here's what it's all about for me…

First, there's the spread of ideas. There are people who have a new idea and just go around talking about their idea. They don't evangelize, per se, but just go around talking about it. They feel strongly, they share freely, they are passionate, and they just keep on going. Had I known Corey Haines before I started writing this book, he might very well have been the inspiration. For those who don't know Corey, I'll tell you that while I was writing this book he was traveling around, talking about and practicing Software Craftsmanship. He would travel to a place where someone was willing to host him and allow him to do some pair programming with them. When he left, he left a little bit of the light of Software Craftsmanship.

The folks he has worked with continue to spread the light, becoming Corey's Lamplighters and Shadowpushers.

If you examine many of the most compelling and change-inducing ideas that have come to you, you may well find that you learned about them on Twitter or Facebook or through email. You may have heard someone speak at a conference, or been involved in a conversation. There was a moment, I suspect, when you had that moment of "Oh! This idea is important to me." That's certainly happened to me more than once.

I became fascinated with a simple idea about the spread of ideas, and that was the germination of this book.

Second, there's the idea of stepping outside of one's barriers in the service of something compelling. Ham is in search of the Lightbringer, and that leads him to do things and think things that no one else has. Ham's commitment and eagerness are his drivers, and along the way, he changes the world. For me, as I discovered Ham's journey, I became aware of him as a person and explorer. His willingness to do something because it needed to be done in service to his quest evolved and unfolded as I wrote. His effect on the people who moved into and out of his immediate circle of influence was directly related to his willingness and his commitment.

In my work – both as a leader and as a coach – I've found too many people who start with their limitations and boundaries, the things they believe they can't do or won't succeed at. My greatest successes have been with those people who were able to see that those limitations were artificial and self-imposed.

In the Agile Software Development community, I've had several people tell me that they see this book as the story of Agile adoption and enablement. When a team or organization first moves to adopt the Agile methodologies, practices, and principles, they are in many ways moving into unknown territories. They are almost certainly stepping outside of the boundaries of their comfort zones. Is this book about Agile adoption? It is, if that's what it is for you.

The same is true in other communities, disciplines, and contexts.

I hope this book made you think. More than that, I hope that it made you think and then take action on what you thought.

If it did, drop me a note.

And even if it didn't, I hope you enjoyed Ham's journey and the ideas it represents.

Regards,

...Doc
...Doc@AnotherThought.com

Reaching for Goals

My daughter Sami reminded me of this on Facebook today:

"It is a paradoxical but profoundly true and important principle of life that the most likely way to reach a goal is to be aiming not at that goal itself but at some more ambitious goal beyond it." Arnold Toynbee

It got me to thinking about Ham, and how he maintained his focus on finding the Lightbringer. Not on making a water bag or a walking staff or making fire, but on the larger, more ambitious goal of finding the Lightbringer.

And along the way, in service to that larger goal, he achieved many smaller goals and helped others to reach smaller goals.

ABOUT THE AUTHOR

Doc List grew up in a family of psychotherapists. His father's father, his father, his father's sister, and his older brother were/are psychologists. His two younger sisters hold MSW degrees and are psychotherapists. His mother retired from her first career at 60 and became a psychotherapist. He's had a couple of stepmothers who were psychotherapists as well. As a result Doc grew up in an environment in which is was natural to ask "why do you feel that way?" or "what do you think you can do about that?" He likes to say that other families had family meetings and the List family had group therapy.

After graduating from college with a Bachelor's Degree in Clinical Psychology, Doc moved from New York City to San Francisco. He met Debbie, who ultimately became his wife (42 years as of this writing). After marrying but before children (they made four of them - Seth, Matt, Sami, and Sydney) Doc fell into a job in the software industry. While working at his first startup, Doc and his two older children began the study/practice of Shotokan Karate. Doc holds a 3rd degree black belt.

For the next 40 years Doc pursued technology, management, leadership, facilitation, professional speaking, entrepreneurship, and photography. Today Doc is an Enterprise Agile Coach and

Enterprise Business Agility Strategist as well as a professional photographer providing fine art portraits, headshots, and dance photography.

9 780999 832219